The Class Pet
from the
Black Lagoon

by Mike Thaler · pictures by Jared Lee

CLASS PET

SCHOLASTIC INC.

New York   Toronto   London   Auckland   Sydney
Mexico City   New Delhi   Hong Kong   Buenos Aires

To the wonderful students
at Cherokee Elementary
and to their loving librarian, Michelle Sisk,
and their principal, Mrs. Elizabeth Spurlock.
—M.T.

For Buster, Shane, Brucey, Boots, Ginger, and Spanky...
all dear companions past and present.
—J.L.

ISBN 0-439-55718-6

Text copyright © 2003 by Mike Thaler.
Illustrations copyright © 2003 by Jared D. Lee Studio, Inc.

12 11 10 9 8 7 6   4 5 6 7 8/0

Printed in the U.S.A.
First printing, October 2003

Mrs. Green is bringing in a class pet.

She won't tell us what it is.

She's bringing it from home—her home!

I wonder what it will look like.

Will it have spots?

Will it have stripes?

Will it have splotches?

Will it have feathers?

Will it have fur?

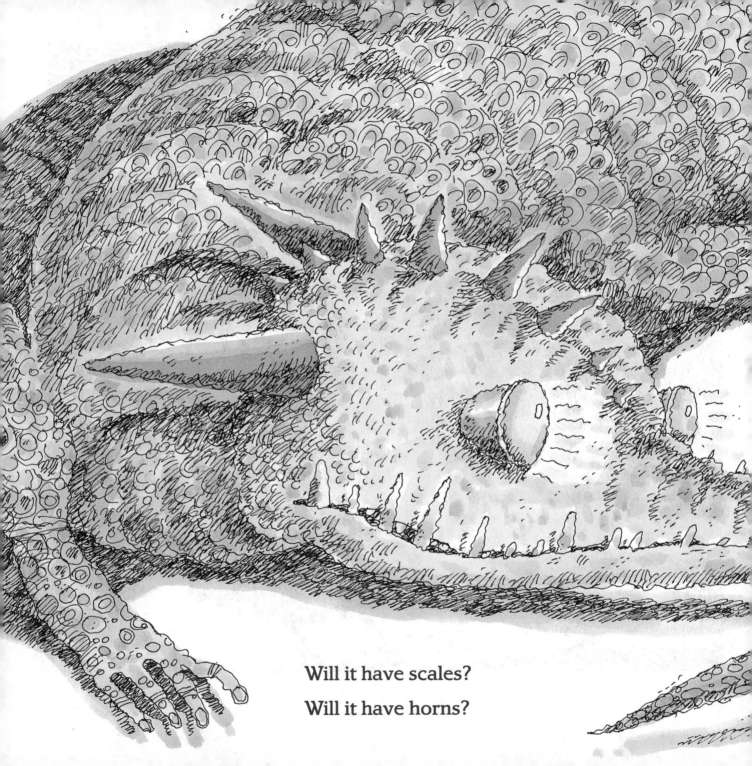

Will it have scales?

Will it have horns?

Will it have headlights?

Will it wiggle?

Will it walk?

THUMP
THUMP

Will it hop? Will it jump?

Or will it just sit there like a lump?

 Mrs. Green says she's bringing a cage, too!

Don't lions live in cages?

Will it be wild?

Will it be mild?

Can we pet it?

Can we hold it?

Can we take it for a walk?

And what will it eat? Lettuce? Custard? Us?

Maybe it will be a *carnivore* . . . and eat cars!

How many legs will it have? And how many teeth?

Two, four, six, eight . . . what will we appreciate?

Maybe it will be two animals stuck together like a *kangarooster* . . .

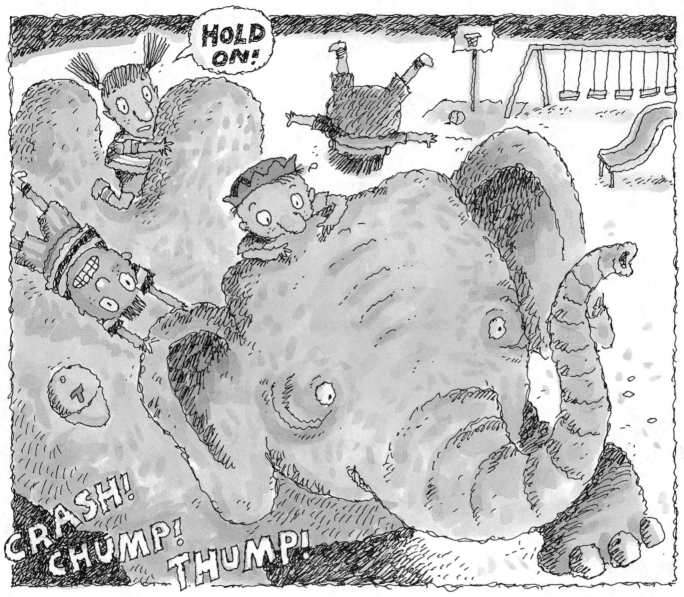

. . . or a *camelephant*!

Maybe it will be a big bug or just a big blob.

I'm scared!

Mrs. Green says its first name is Dina.

I hope its last name isn't *Saur*.

Well, here they come.

Two shadows cover the door.

In steps Mrs. Green with a hamster.

It doesn't look too ferocious.

In fact, it looks as scared as we looked.

I'm going to hug it and let it know that it doesn't have anything to be afraid of.